leapfrog

Felix
on the Move

First published in 2000
Franklin Watts
96 Leonard Street
London
EC2A 4XD

Franklin Watts Australia
45-51 Huntley Street
Alexandria
NSW 2015

A CIP catalogue record for this book is available
from the British Library.

ISBN 0 7496 3731 5 (hbk)
ISBN 0 7496 4387 0 (pbk)

Series Editor: Louise John
Series Advisor: Dr Barrie Wade
Series Designer: Jason Anscomb

Printed in China

Felix
on the Move

by Maeve Friel

Illustrated by Beccy Blake

FRANKLIN WATTS

LONDON • SYDNEY

Felix was a very happy cat.

He liked sitting on the
window sill ...

and napping in secret places.

He liked playing in the garden.

And he liked his family
so much, he gave them a
present every day.

One morning, a big van arrived at the house.

Out went the sofa where
Felix liked to have his
afternoon naps.

12

Out went the rug that he sharpened his claws on.

Out went the beds, the television and the fridge.

Worst of all, out went his yellow, plastic bowl.

Felix was not a happy cat.

Soon, there was nothing left but a cat basket.

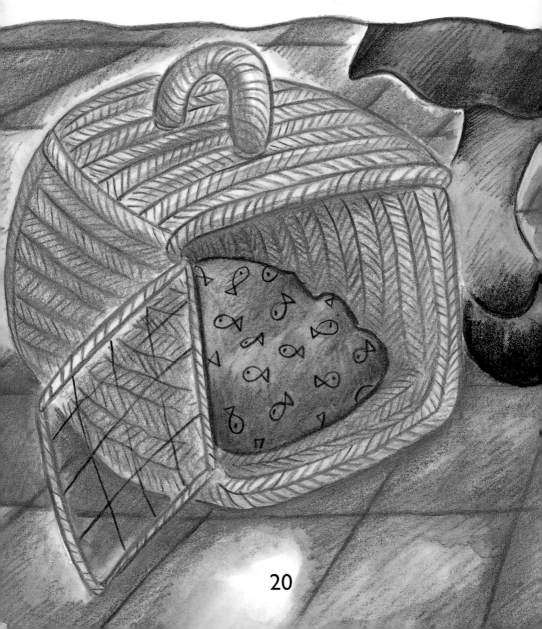

"I'm not getting in that," growled Felix.

But he did!

Felix was all alone in an empty room.

In came the sofa,
the rug, the television
and the fridge.

In came his yellow, plastic bowl.

28

Best of all, in came the family.

Felix settled down for a nap.

"This is the life," he purred.

"Home again!"

Leapfrog has been specially designed to fit the requirements of the National Literacy Strategy. It offers real books for beginning readers by top authors and illustrators.

There are 25 Leapfrog stories to choose from:

The Bossy Cockerel

Written by Margaret Nash,
illustrated by Elisabeth Moseng

Bill's Baggy Trousers

Written by Susan Gates,
illustrated by Anni Axworthy

Mr Spotty's Potty

Written by Hilary Robinson,
illustrated by Peter Utton

Little Joe's Big Race

Written by Andy Blackford,
illustrated by Tim Archbold

The Little Star

Written by Deborah Nash,
illustrated by Richard Morgan

The Cheeky Monkey

Written by Anne Cassidy,
illustrated by Lisa Smith

Selfish Sophie

Written by Damian Kelleher,
illustrated by Georgie Birkett

Recycled!

Written by Jillian Powell,
illustrated by Amanda Wood

Felix on the Move

Written by Maeve Friel,
illustrated by Beccy Blake

Pippa and Poppa

Written by Anne Cassidy,
illustrated by Philip Norman

Jack's Party

Written by Ann Bryant,
illustrated by Claire Henley

The Best Snowman

Written by Margaret Nash,
illustrated by Jörg Saupe

Eight Enormous Elephants

Written by Penny Dolan,
illustrated by Leo Broadley

Mary and the Fairy

Written by Penny Dolan,
illustrated by Deborah Allwright

The Crying Princess

Written by Anne Cassidy,
illustrated by Colin Paine

Cinderella

Written by Barrie Wade,
illustrated by Julie Monks

The Three Little Pigs

Written by Maggie Moore,
illustrated by Rob Hefferan

The Three Billy Goats Gruff

Written by Barrie Wade,
illustrated by Nicola Evans

Goldilocks and the Three Bears

Written by Barrie Wade,
illustrated by Kristina Stephenson

Jack and the Beanstalk

Written by Maggie Moore,
illustrated by Steve Cox

Little Red Riding Hood

Written by Maggie Moore,
illustrated by Paula Knight

Jasper and Jess

Written by Anne Cassidy,
illustrated by François Hall

The Lazy Scarecrow

Written by Jillian Powell,
illustrated by Jayne Coughlin

The Naughty Puppy

Written by Jillian Powell,
illustrated by Summer Durantz

Freddie's Fears

Written by Hilary Robinson,
illustrated by Ross Collins